Harry and His Bucket Full of Dinosaurs

The Dreaded Fluffosaurus

Based on the original stories created by
Ian Whybrow and Adrian Reynolds

PUFFIN BOOKS
Published by the Penguin Group: London, New York,
Australia, Canada, India, Ireland, New Zealand and South Africa
Penguin Books Ltd, Registered Offices: 80 Strand, London WC2R 0RL, England

puffinbooks.com

First published 2008
1 3 5 7 9 10 8 6 4 2

Made and printed in China
ISBN: 978–0–141–50184–0

D0652946

Harry's friend Charley had come over to play. She had brought her new pet kitten, Buster.

"Wow!" said Harry. "He's so little!"

They took Buster into the garden where Harry's dinosaurs were playing.

"What is it?" asked Steggy.

"It's a new toy!" exclaimed Pterence.

"It's not a new toy," said Taury. "It's a new dinosaur! The dreaded Fluffosaurus!"

They crept towards Buster to get a closer look.

Buster was just a little kitten but to the dinosaurs he was huge. And he had a mouth full of sharp teeth!

"Run!" shouted Taury. They all jumped into the bucket to escape.

But Buster jumped in too . . .
He was on his way to Dino World!
"Don't worry, Charley, I'll get him back," said Harry, and he followed Buster and the dinosaurs to Dino World.
"One, two, three . . . JUMP!"

Harry found the dinosaurs hiding in a cave.

"Don't be frightened!" he laughed. "He's just a little kitten and he's probably really scared. We've got to find him."

But the dinosaurs weren't too sure.

"It'll be like going on safari, tracking the jungle cat!" said Harry.

A safari! Now that did sound fun to the dinosaurs!

They travelled through Dino World in their safari jeep. The jungle was alive with colourful birds and beautiful butterflies. But where was Buster?

Suddenly, a coconut landed on Trike's horn.

"Mmm," he said, slurping coconut milk.

They all looked up to see why the coconut had fallen. There, perched high up in the palm tree above, was Buster.

"Buster!" Harry called. The dinosaurs couldn't believe it. In Dino World, Buster was tiny!

Patsy was tall enough to reach Buster, but before she could get him down, he had grabbed a hanging vine and was swinging off through the trees.

"Oh no!" shouted Harry. "We've got to catch him!" He turned the jeep around and chased after Buster.

When they spotted him, Buster was walking across a very thin straw-bridge. "Careful, Buster!" called Pterence.

"We'll come and get you!" Taury called to Buster.
Harry edged along the straw-bridge carefully,
followed by Taury and the others.

They formed a long, strong dino chain. Steggy was at
the end with his tail wrapped tightly round a tree.

Then, one by one, Harry and the dinosaurs fell from the bridge.
Only Steggy's tail was stopping them all from plunging into
the Orange Juice River below.

But the weight of the dinosaurs was too much for the tree.
The whole thing uprooted and fell into the river, along with
Harry, the dinosaurs and little Buster.

They all scrambled on to the back of an ice-cube.
"There's Buster!" shouted Harry, pointing downstream.
Buster was floating away on the back of the straw,
heading straight for a waterfall!

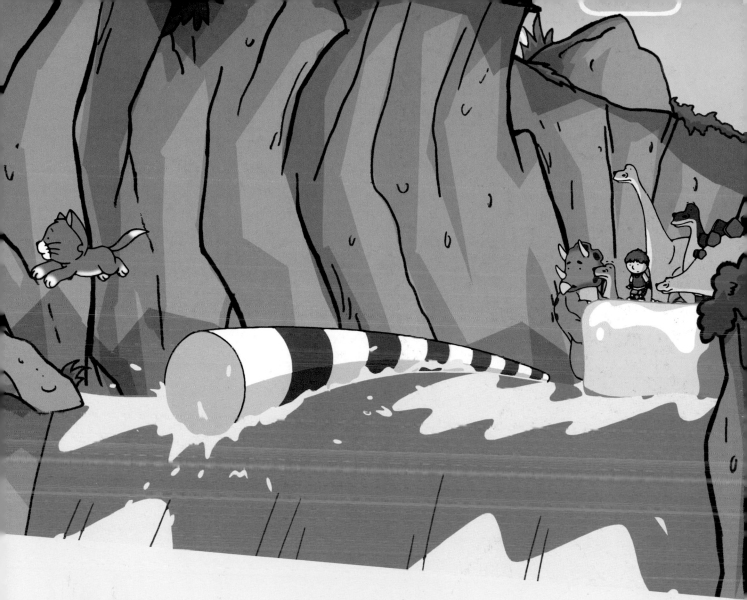

"Buster! Look out!" shouted Harry.

Buster jumped to safety just in time, but Harry and his dinosaurs were right behind him . . .

"Nooooo!"

they all yelled, as they plunged over the edge.

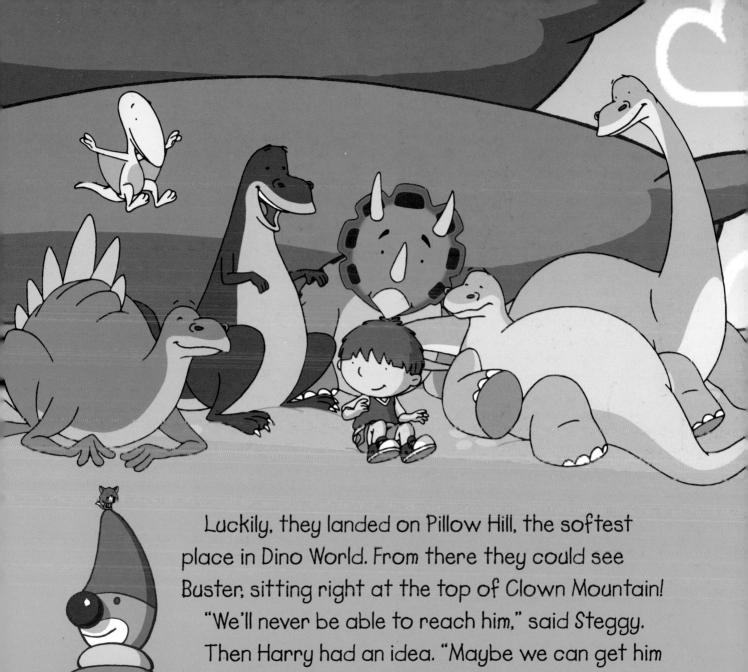

Luckily, they landed on Pillow Hill, the softest place in Dino World. From there they could see Buster, sitting right at the top of Clown Mountain! "We'll never be able to reach him," said Steggy. Then Harry had an idea. "Maybe we can get him to come to us!"

Harry knew that kittens love milk, and there was plenty of coconut milk in Dino World. He poured some into a saucer and made a cage from drinking straws.

"Buster won't be able to resist," said Harry.

When Harry had finished, he went to hide with the others.
"Here, kitty kitty," they all called.
Buster heard them and began to climb down . . .

Harry's plan worked perfectly!
Soon Buster was busy lapping up the milk.
He was safe at last.

Harry picked up Buster.
"You're a little kitten," he said.
"But you're big trouble!"
Buster seemed to agree.
He gave Harry a big wet lick.

"Buster! They found you!" Charley cheered, as Buster landed back in the garden. Everyone was delighted he was back safe and sound. And it was all thanks to Harry.